# Dinner for Fox

First published in 2008 by
Franklin Watts
338 Euston Road
London
NW1 3BH

Franklin Watts Australia
Level 17/207 Kent Street
Sydney
NSW 2000



A CIP catalogue record for this book is available from the British Library.

ISBN 978 0 7496 7887 6 (hbk)
ISBN 978 0 7496 7893 7 (pbk)

**Series Editor:** Jackie Hamley
**Series Advisor:** Dr Hilary Minns
**Series Designer:** Peter Scoulding

Printed in China

Franklin Watts is a division of
Hachette Children's Books,
an Hachette Livre UK company.

For Daniel, with love – A.C.L.

For Lia and Mark, with love – C.J.

# Dinner for Fox

by Caryn Jenner

Illustrated by Anna C. Leplar

W
FRANKLIN WATTS
LONDON•SYDNEY

**Caryn Jenner**

"This is my daughter, Lia. We sometimes see foxes in the city. Lia always wonders where the foxes are going. She helped me to write this story."



**Anna C. Leplar**

"I live in Iceland with my family and my dog, Tess. Foxes here have brown or grey fur in summer, but in winter their fur is white."

Fox was hungry.

He sniffed the air.
He smelled dinner!

Fox went to look in a garden.

Where was dinner?

Not here.

He went to look
in the field.

Where was dinner?

Not here either.

Fox sniffed the air again. His dinner was getting closer.

He went to look
in the park.

At last, Fox found his dinner!

# Notes for adults

**TADPOLES** are structured to provide support for newly independent readers. The stories may also be used by adults for sharing with young children.

Starting to read alone can be daunting. **TADPOLES** help by providing visual support and repeating words and phrases. These books will both develop confidence and encourage reading and rereading for pleasure.

**If you are reading this book with a child, here are a few suggestions:**

1. Make reading fun! Choose a time to read when you and the child are relaxed and have time to share the story.
2. Talk about the story before you start reading. Look at the cover and the blurb. What might the story be about? Why might the child like it?
3. Encourage the child to reread the story, and to retell the story in their own words, using the illustrations to remind them what has happened.
4. Discuss the story and see if the child can relate it to their own experience, or perhaps compare it to another story they know.
5. Give praise! Remember that small mistakes need not always be corrected.

**If you enjoyed this book, why not try another TADPOLES story?**

**Sammy's Secret**
978 0 7496 6890 7

**Stroppy Poppy**
978 0 7496 6893 8

**I'm Taller Than You!**
978 0 7496 6894 5

**Leo's New Pet**
978 0 7496 6891 4

**Mop Top**
978 0 7946 6895 2

**Charlie and the Castle**
978 0 7496 6896 9

**Over the Moon!**
978 0 7496 6897 6

**Five Teddy Bears**
978 0 7496 7292 8

**My Sister is a Witch!**
978 0 7496 6898 3

**Little Troll**
978 0 7496 7293 5

**The Sad Princess**
978 0 7496 7294 2

**Runny Honey**
978 0 7496 7295 9

**Dog Knows Best**
978 0 7496 7297 3

**Sam's Sunflower**
978 0 7496 7298 0

**My Big New Bed**
978 0 7496 7156 3 (hbk)
978 0 7496 7299 7 (pbk)

**My Auntie Susan**
978 0 7496 7157 0 (hbk)
978 0 7496 7300 0 (pbk)

**Bad Luck, Lucy!**
978 0 7496 7158 7 (hbk)
978 0 7496 7302 4 (pbk)

**At the End of the Garden**
978 0 7496 7159 4 (hbk)
978 0 7496 7303 1 (pbk)

**Bertie and the Big Balloon**
978 0 7496 7161 7 (hbk)
978 0 7496 7305 5 (pbk)

**Pirate Pete**
978 0 7496 7160 0 (hbk)
978 0 7496 7304 8 (pbk)